"You need to save up,"
said Mum.

Evan looked at the money
in his jar.

"Will you help me?"
he said to Mum.
"I need to save up."

Evan helped Mum
wash the car.

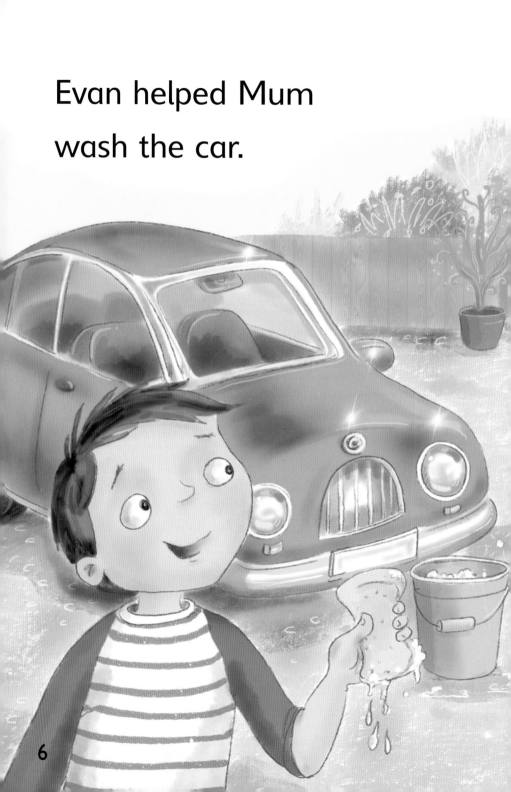

Mum gave him some money.

Evan looked at the money
in his jar.

"Can I buy the rocket now?"
he said.

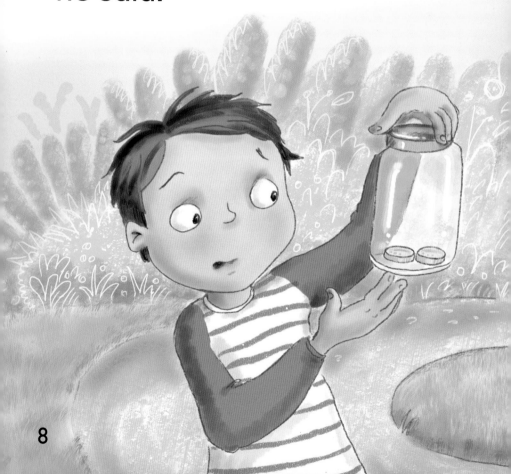

"Not yet," said Mum.

"You need to save up."

Evan helped Mum
carry the shopping.

Mum gave him some money.

Evan looked at the money
in his jar.

"Can I buy the rocket now?"
he said.

"Not yet," said Mum.
"You need to save up."

Evan helped Mum
dig the garden.

Mum gave him some money.

Evan looked at the money in his jar.

"Can I buy the rocket now?" he said.

"Yes," said Mum.
"We can go to the shop
and get the rocket."

Evan went to the shop
to get the rocket.

Evan looked at
a skateboard ...

Story trail

Start at the beginning of the story trail. Ask your child to retell the story in their own words, pointing to each picture in turn to recall the sequence of events.

Start

Independent Reading

This series is designed to provide an opportunity for your child to read on their own. These notes are written for you to help your child choose a book and to read it independently.

In school, your child's teacher will often be using reading books which have been banded to support the process of learning to read.

Use the book band colour your child is reading in school to help you make a good choice. *Evan's Rocket* is a good choice for children reading at Yellow Band in their classroom to read independently.

The aim of independent reading is to read this book with ease, so that your child enjoys the story and relates it to their own experiences.

About the book

Evan really wants to buy the rocket he sees in the shop, but he doesn't have enough money. He does some jobs for Mum and learns to save up for it.

Before reading

Help your child to learn how to make good choices by asking: "Why did you choose this book? Why do you think you will enjoy it?" Look at the cover together and ask: "What do you think the story will be about?" Support your child to think of what they already know about the story context. Read the title aloud and ask: "Do you think Evan would like to have the rocket in the shop window? Why do you think that?"

Remind your child that they can try to sound out the letters to make a word if they get stuck.

Decide together whether your child will read the story independently or read it aloud to you. When books are short, as at Yellow Band, your child may wish to do both!

During reading

If reading aloud, support your child if they hesitate or ask for help by telling the word. Remind your child of what they know and what they can do independently.
If reading to themselves, remind your child that they can come and ask for your help if stuck.

After reading

Support comprehension by asking your child to tell you about the story. Use the story trail to encourage your child to retell the story in the right sequence, in their own words.
Help your child think about the messages in the book that go beyond the story and ask: "Do you think Evan will try to save up and buy the skateboard he sees at the end of the story? Why / why not?"
Give your child a chance to respond to the story: "Did you have a favourite part? Have you ever had something that you really wanted and you saved up for? What was it?"

Extending learning

Help your child understand the story structure by using the same sentence patterns and adding some new elements. "Let's make up a new story about Evan buying the skateboard. 'Can I buy the skateboard?' said Evan. 'Not yet,' said Mum. 'You need to save up.' Evan helped Mum fold the clothes. Mum gave him some money. Now you try. What will Evan want to buy in your story?"
Your child's teacher will be talking about punctuation at Yellow Band. On a few of the pages, check your child can recognise capital letters, question marks, exclamation marks and full stops by asking them to point these out.

Franklin Watts
First published in Great Britain in 2019
by The Watts Publishing Group

Copyright © The Watts Publishing Group 2019

Series Editors: Jackie Hamley and Melanie Palmer
Series Advisors: Dr Sue Bodman and Glen Franklin
Series Designer: Peter Scoulding

A CIP catalogue record for this book is
available from the British Library.

ISBN 978 1 4451 6786 2 (hbk)
ISBN 978 1 4451 6788 6 (pbk)
ISBN 978 1 4451 6787 9 (library ebook)

Printed in China

Franklin Watts
An imprint of
Hachette Children's Group
Part of The Watts Publishing Group
Carmelite House
50 Victoria Embankment
London EC4Y 0DZ

An Hachette UK Company
www.hachette.co.uk

www.franklinwatts.co.uk